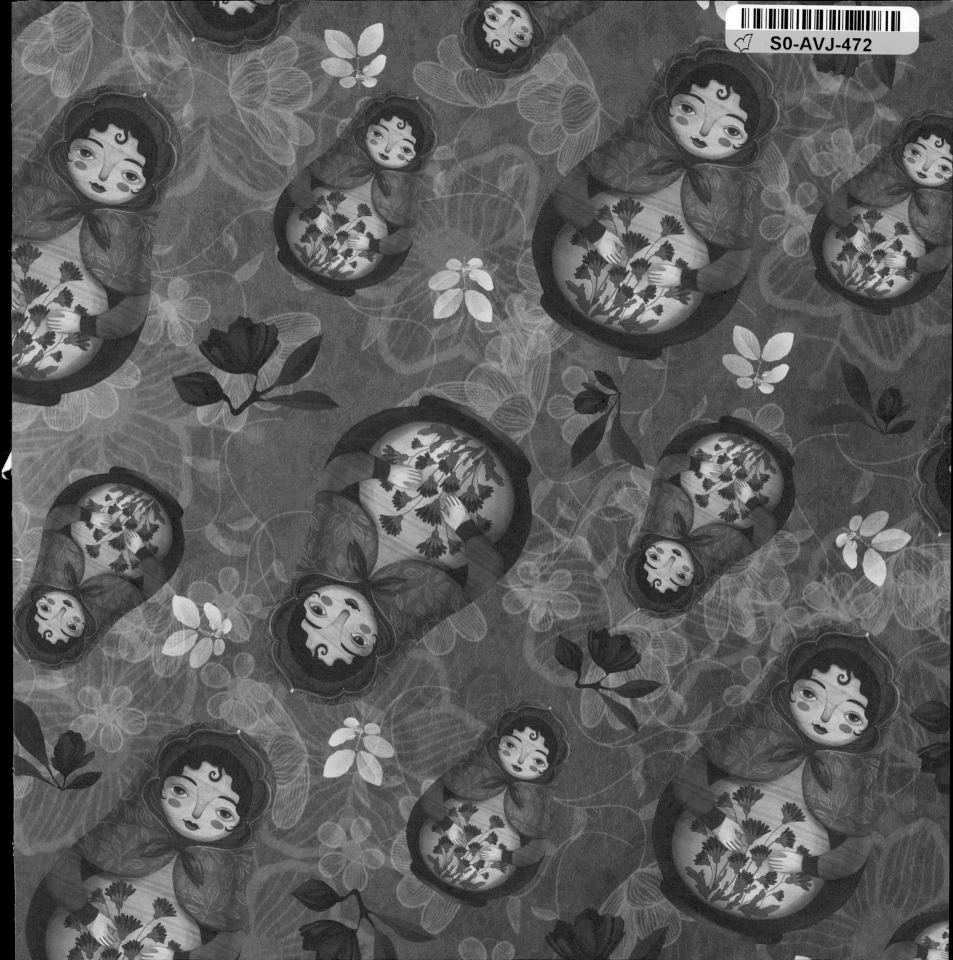

For both my Babas and Karina.

Baba means Grandmother in Ukrainian, and Babushka is "little Baba."

Holodomor is a Ukrainian compound word made up of the words holod, which means hunger, and mar, which means plague. It was estimated that 14.5 million deaths occurred from actions of the soviet communist party—which the author of this book, in memory of people affected by hunger between 1929 and 1933, refuses to write in capital letters.

"Tell me a story, Babushka," said Karina, looking at the bread dough being kneaded by Baba.

"Would you like a story about a princess, Karina?"

"Maybe one of those stories about a princess and monsters, Baba."

"Once upon a time, there was a little girl in Ukraine. She was poor of money but rich of soul. She lived in a little house with a thatched roof. It was a cottage like those from fairy tales."

"There is no fairy tale with a cottage, Baba."

"Isn't there, Karina?"

"No. But there should be, Babushka. I would like to live in an adorable cottage."

Baba smiled. "The little girl had a small flower and vegetable garden where potatoes and the world's biggest cabbages grew. She and her family were happy living there, but only until the day the monsters arrived in the little town."

"What did they do?"

"They took away the Ukrainians' freedom. At first, the monsters stole all the grains produced in Ukraine. Many Ukrainians became sick and even died because there was no food. Then, the monsters wanted more grains."

"Why didn't the Ukrainians hide the grains?"

"The monsters said they would kill anyone who hid their grains."

"What happened to the little girl?"

"Her beautiful cottage was invaded by the monsters, like other cottages. The little girl hid herself under the bed. Years later, these horrible happenings would be called the Holodomor, my darling."

"Did the monsters find her?"

"Yes. They took her whole family, including the other families, to a horrible camp in Siberia."

"What happened to them, Baba?"

"The adults had to work for the monsters, and the children were separated from their parents. But one day in Siberia, the little girl found a matryoshka under her mattress on the floor. Do you know matryoshka dolls, Karina?"

"Those sets of painted wooden dolls, which can be opened, and they nest inside one another?"

"That's it. Can you imagine? There were no pillows, but a matryoshka appeared under her mattress. She saw the other girls also hiding matryoshkas. She opened the first doll, then the second, third, and fourth. On the fifth matryoshka, there was a message."

"A message of rescue!"

"Yes, it was written that the monsters would be in a meeting that dawn.

The message said they should not make noise when a woman arrives to help them escape. The children stayed still at night. The rescue operation saved all those children."

"What happened next?"

"They walked through a forest at night and boarded a train. The train with the little girl would leave soon. But 'to where?' she thought and then prayed. She was carrying a scarf."

"Was the scarf in her hands, like those girls that shake scarves to say goodbye in movies, Baba?"

"No, Karina. Her scarf was far from her hands and goodbyes. She tied it on her head. She was also wearing a skirt that dragged on the floor.

She was just a little girl, so much smaller than her skirt! That skirt was long, so it would last longer—maybe all her childhood."

"I heard that, in the old days, poor people bought longer skirts to last longer, Baba."

"That's right, darling. She was trying to look through a crack in the wagon. Do you know, Karina, those trains departing with young girls waving goodbyes with their scarves had windows, but trains departing with girls with scarves tied on their heads had cracks?"

"Poor girl, Baba!"

"Poor girl . . . She looked through a crack in the wagon and understood she was leaving her past life behind forever."

"What came next for the little girl? Where was she going?"

"What would come, she had no idea. Maybe in the new place there would be no gunshots and hunger—and the long skirt could maybe last all her childhood. She was a bit scared of the unknown future, but she remembered that her past was scarier than any future. She looked through the crack for the last time. She hugged her matryoshka and her memories.
Then, to the unknown, she departed."

"And then, Baba?"

"Years later, in another country, the little girl is now a happy old lady, kneading bread dough and telling a true story to her granddaughter."

"That's a very happy ending. You're a princess, Baba."

# Carola Schmidt

lives in Curitiba, Brazil. Called Carolina at birth, she was nicknamed Carola by her Baba (grandmother) Amelia, whose mother emigrated to Brazil from Ukraine. Wanting to know more about her family's homeland, Carola traveled to present-day Ukraine. She returned understanding that our memories are like a favorite blanket creating a cozy feeling of belonging. It was in Ukraine where she decided to write this story—a tale of how she imagined her missing family history and their escape from a difficult time long ago. Today, Carola writes children's books and works as a pediatric oncology pharmacist, helping children going through cancer treatments.

# Anita Barghigiani

was born near Pisa, Italy, on September 24, 1987. After graduating from the Academy of Fine Arts of Florence, she took part in many festivals as a scenographer and photographer. In 2010 she attended the Bologna Children's Book Fair for the first time and fell in love with children's books. She then decided to study illustration and entertainment design at NEMO Academy of Digital Arts. Since then, she's worked as an illustrator for publishers and as a painter and decorator for Dolce & Gabbana. She currently lives in Florence, Italy, where she works, plays the guitar, and actively helps animals as a volunteer.

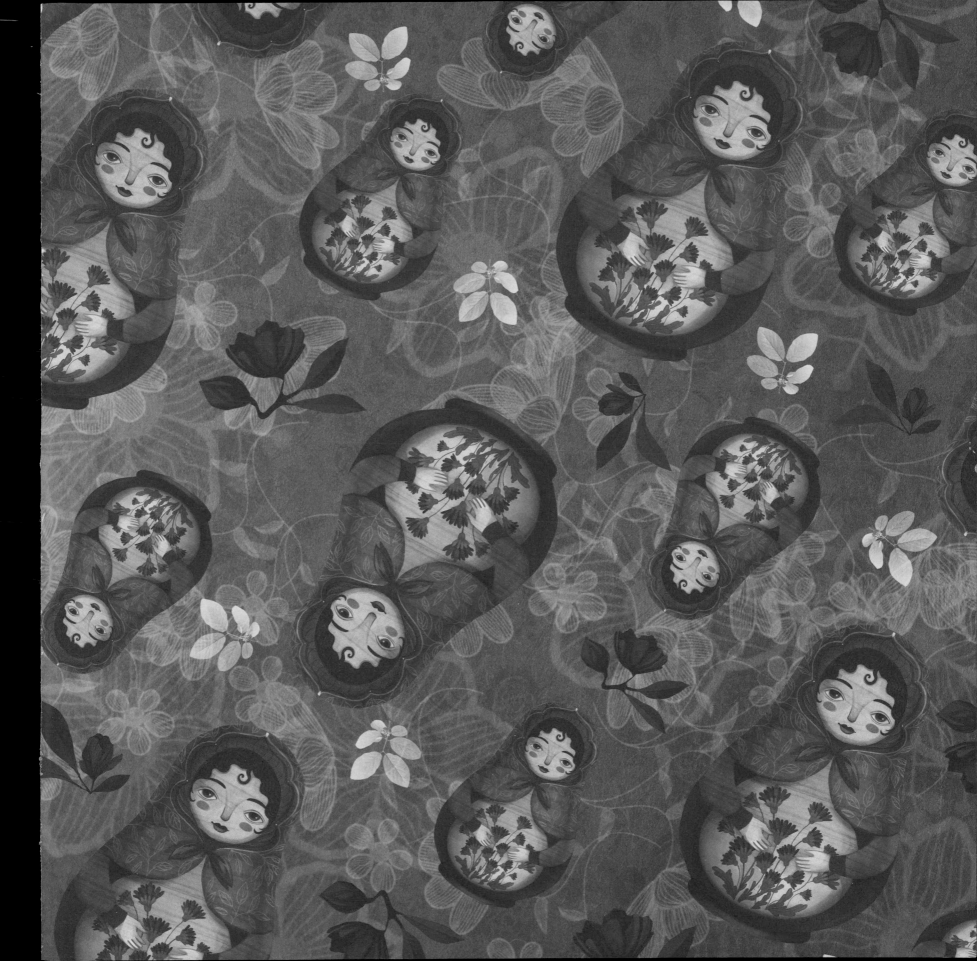

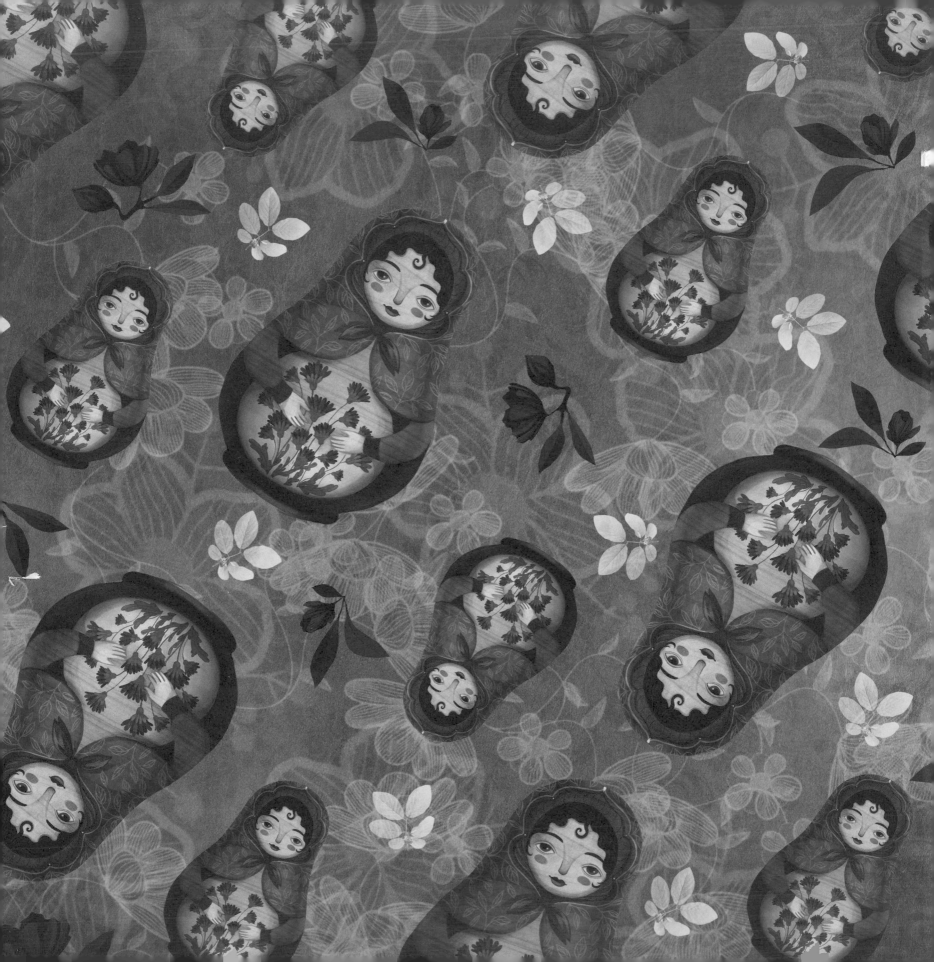